This book belongs to:

How To Explain Christmas To Chickens

A Modestly Illustrated Story by

John Spiers

Copyright © John Spiers, 2020

All rights reserved. No part of this book may be reproduced or used in any manner without prior written permission from the author except for the use of brief quotations in a book review.

This book must be considered a work of fiction because the author was not a direct observer of all that happened. He relied on the accounts of his chickens to fill in those missing details. While he trusts them for their honesty, there could be a few places where his imagination may have gotten the best of him.

Any resemblance to actual persons, living or dead, is entirely coincidental. Any resemblance to the actual chickens who call the author's backyard their home is entirely purposeful. This book would never have been written without the inspiration of Blanche and the assistance of Gracie, Bessie, Pearl, Emily, and Amelia.

ISBN 978-1-0879-2187-7

First Edition November 2020

Dedication

For Blanche,
Pearl's very best friend ever,
who left us one Easter Sunday
with lessons about giving
which became alive in our hearts
one Christmas morning

Contents

Preface	vii
Our Backyard Garden	ix
Blanche And Pearl	1
Hatching A New Idea	4
Pearl's Comedy Coop	7
The Bottle Cap Lady	12
Under The Camellias	17
No More Jokes To Tell	22
A Wondrous Place	27
Secrets And Presents	34
The Most Silent Pearl Ever	39
A Happy Merry Christmas	46
About The Author	52
About This Book	53

Preface

This story occurs in the intersection where the world of people meets the world of chickens. Intersections are interesting places where the unexpected can happen. Chickens can talk with people who truly love them. They can also dance ballet, put on backyard comedy shows, and even draw pictures.

Christmas is an intersection too. It is where the world of what is seen meets the world of what is unseen and where the world of the ordinary meets the world of the extraordinary.

Sometimes when worlds intersect, a miracle occurs. It may be grand and brilliantly glorious, or it may be soft and barely noticeable. But it will happen nevertheless.

This book is about what happened one Christmas when the world of my little white chicken named Pearl intersected the world of The Bottle Cap Lady.

One late fall day while I was raking leaves, Pearl had asked me about all of the decorations in our neighborhood. But how do you explain Christmas to a chicken?

When you don't answer a chicken's question, the chicken will try to find the answer anyway. The world can be a very dangerous place for chickens, especially curious chickens.

Hopefully this book will serve as a guide to help you explain Christmas to your own chickens so they will not go wandering around your neighborhood looking for their own answers. If you will read this story to your chickens, I believe their curiosity will be satisfied, and they will wait peacefully for you to bring them their Christmas morning treats.

In this book, you will find both happy things and sad things because a chicken's life can be that way. You will also find secrets, promises, and, of course, a simple everyday miracle or two.

John Spiers
April 17, 2020 - Hatchday for Blanche and Pearl

Our Backyard Garden

A backyard garden is a perfect place for chickens and a most wondrous place for friends. Pearl helped make this drawing. You can help too by adding plenty of bright and beautiful garden colors if you would like.

Blanche And Pearl

Pearl was excited. "Today is the day my new life will begin!" she said although there were no other chickens nearby to hear her.

It was the day she was going to lay her first egg. "Do I look any different yet? I just know I'm going to look different."

"You look much happier, Pearl," I said. "You truly do."

Pearl had always been different from the day she hatched. She was hardly ever quiet or hardly ever still. Calamities and mishaps always seemed to follow her. She would accidentally bump into the water bottle or turn over the food bowl.

None of the others understood her or wanted to be around her. Blanche was her only friend from the day they had hatched together. Blanche loved Pearl without needing to understand her. That is just what friends do.

They had travelled from the hatchery to the post office in the same ventilated box as over a dozen other chicks. The post office is where chickens come from when you live in the city.

Then just the two of them had travelled together in the same small shoebox from the post office to my home where Gracie and Bessie were waiting. Their original hatchmates had all gone off to homes in the country to raise their own families. They would no longer be the only chickens in my backyard once Blanche and Pearl had outgrown their brooder box.

From the beginning, Blanche loved Pearl, and Pearl looked to Blanche as her substitute mother hen. She did not realize Blanche was just as new to the world as she was.

They shared a special bond, partly because they both had pure white feathers, but mostly because they were the only two raised by themselves.

They only ever had each other.

Every day, Gracie or Bessie would ask her, "Why can't you just be a good normal chicken?" Pearl tried the best she knew how, but she still got herself into trouble. She still got pecked.

She hoped once she could lay an egg like everyone else, they would love her the same way Blanche loved her. For Pearl, laying an egg was the biggest mystery of all time.

Once Blanche began laying eggs, she made up a game called Let's Lay An Egg to help Pearl learn what to do. Mostly it kept her curiosity from getting her into trouble with the others.

Blanche told her, "Laying an egg is all about giving. Light and Life and Love are all about giving too."

After Pearl laid her first egg, she rolled it out of the coop so everyone could see it. Fortunately it landed on the morning's fresh straw. But on the way down the chicken ladder, she tripped and fell on her egg. It made a gooey mess.

Everyone gathered around her. She made her goofiest face and held up her foot so the gooey egg could drip off. She closed her eyes and waited to be pecked. To her surprise, everyone clucked with laughter instead of pecking her for being clumsy.

After I gave her a warm bath, she joined the others in hunting for grasshoppers. They were so close together no insect could possibly escape. Maybe Pearl really would fit in at last.

When I looked up, I saw our neighbor, The Bottle Cap Lady, standing quietly where the driveway meets the street. Maybe she too was waiting for her own wonderful new life to begin.

Hatching A New Idea

That night after the others had fallen asleep, Blanche huddled closer to Pearl in their corner and whispered, "I am not feeling well. I might be sick. I might be very sick. I might not get well."

"Don't be silly, Blanche," Pearl whispered back. "You are already as big as Bessie. Soon you will be as big as Gracie, maybe bigger. Then we can have the best of everything. You have to be well."

Then Blanche did something she thought she would never do. She pecked Pearl so hard several feathers came out. "This is serious!" she said.

Gracie and Bessie woke up. Even the dog next door woke up and started barking.

Pearl's big day had not gone at all like she had hoped. Losing her first egg was bad enough, but losing Blanche would be the worst. She was definitely going to need a new plan. It had to be one that would give them both a wonderful new life.

Pearl got her new plan the next day when everyone was practicing ballet. It was the first time Blanche and Pearl had worn the ballet slippers and tutus I had made for them to match the ones Gracie and Bessie already had.

As they started dancing, Blanche had trouble with one of her ballet slippers, and we started to hear it flapping and clopping on her foot.

She tried to fix it but couldn't because her tutu kept getting in the way. The awful noise continued to get louder. She tried to find a graceful way out, but there was none. Pearl disappeared, and Blanche felt even worse.

Suddenly Pearl reappeared with one of her ballet slippers on top of her head and tied under her chin. She held her bare foot up in the air and started waggling it in time to the music. "Do-Dah! Do-Dah!" she began singing over and over while hopping around. Everyone stopped dancing and began laughing.

No one was looking at Blanche or her mangled homemade ballet slipper. Pearl had rescued her from embarrassment in the silliest way possible. Even Gracie, who always takes ballet very seriously, was laughing.

"Hold it, Sweeties!" I said, looking at Pearl and then Blanche. "What we have here is the biggest ballet mistake ever."

The laughter quickly subsided and everyone looked at me except for Blanche. She hung her head as if she was in for the worst reprimand ever. She began trying to figure out how she would ever survive with no treats for the rest of her life.

"Blanche, this is all my fault," I said.

She looked up at me with surprise.

"I should have realized your special gift for dancing would only be hindered by homemade ballet slippers. We will need to order real ballet slippers for you and matching ones for the others all the way from Paris."

Everyone, even Blanche, nearly fainted from excitement.

"Paris? Paris, France!" said Gracie. "That is the absolute ballet capital of the whole entire world!"

They restarted their practice with everyone dancing barefoot just as Blanche was always meant to dance. And that was when Pearl decided to become a comedian.

Pearl's Comedy Coop

Just as Gracie dreams of being a ballerina with the Paris Opera Ballet, all my chickens have secret ambitions. While I was digging the foundation of a new larger home for everyone in the backyard, Pearl shared hers with me.

"I've been thinking about it for a long time," she said. "If I am a comedian then everyone will love me. Even if they don't love me, at least they will laugh at me. They can't peck me when they are laughing."

"They laugh because you do goofy things sometimes?" I asked.

"Yes. Most of the time I do not intend to do goofy things. They just turn out that way."

Pearl was embarrassed by this. It was like she never quite learned all of the rules of how to be a chicken even though she had tried to copy Blanche as best she could.

She looked up and tried to appear cheerful. "Maybe if they laugh enough, they will learn to love me and be extra kind to us, to Blanche and me." There was tremendous hope in her voice.

"We are getting two new chickens who no longer have a place to live," I said. "That may help. Then, once all of you have settled into this new bigger home, we can temporarily turn our ballet stage into a comedy show stage. You can put on your own show, and we can call it Pearl's Comedy Coop if you'd like."

Pearl was excited. She would have a real audience and maybe the new chickens would understand and love her.

But when Emily and Amelia arrived, things were just the same for Pearl even though Emily was the smallest and looked the most different from all of them. Pearl could not figure it out.

When they had free range time in the garden, Pearl would find scraps of colorful and shiny things. She collected and saved them in a place no one else knew about. She would take them out and carefully arrange them, and that always made her feel calm. Each one held endless possibilities. Maybe they held the secret to starting her wonderful new life.

Tuesdays were her favorite days because it was Trash Truck Day. There were almost always treasures blown out of the trash truck, particularly on windy days.

Sometimes the songbirds brought her glittery or unusual things as well, and then they shared amazing news of the world beyond our garden. Perhaps her wonderful new life was out there somewhere.

Finally I finished the stage decorations for Pearl's show, including a backdrop of Parisian ladies dancing in fancy costumes. Pearl had picked it out herself from one of my art books.

When Pearl's big night arrived, she made everyone line up with their "Admit One" tickets in their beaks. The tickets were mismatched and looked as if they had been torn, thrown away, and glued back together. But that didn't matter. They were real tickets for Pearl's real comedy show. That was what mattered.

I helped everyone to their seats and turned on the lights. Pearl came out and flapped to the top of her stool. There were no calamities or mishaps. She had definitely been practicing.

"Trick or treat!" Pearl called out to the audience as she held up her left foot with its new pink toenail polish. "Smell my feet!" she called out as she switched to holding up her right foot.

Her audience was stunned and silent. They had never seen a chicken or any other animal do something like this, and certainly not with pink toenails.

"Why did the farmer cross the road?" she asked.

"We don't know!" they replied together.

"To feed the chickens!" she said.

Much to my surprise, everyone thought this joke was funny, but it made no sense to me.

"How many farmers does it take to change a lightbulb?" she called out.

No one made a sound.

"Who cares? As long as they feed the chickens!"

Again there was uproarious laughter. Her audience turned and looked at me as if to ask why I didn't understand how funny she was. Her jokes still made no sense to me.

Pearl flipped over onto her back and pretended to be taking a dust bath while telling her next few jokes. Each one was funnier than the one before.

Pearl stretched out her neck, made a goofy face, and acted as if her show was over while she admired her shiny pink toenails. Her audience cheered her on, calling out for more.

"Did you hear about the farmer who forgot to take his umbrella with him when he went outside, but he didn't get wet?"

"No! Why didn't he get wet?" they all said.

"Because it wasn't raining when it was time to..."

The other chickens held their breaths, and just before they were ready to burst out laughing, Pearl cackled, "Feed the chickens!" And then, of course, we all had to laugh.

While everyone was rocking with laughter, I glanced up and saw a light flip on in one of the upstairs windows of The Bottle Cap Lady's house. There was a shadow on the blinds as if someone was standing there and watching the show too.

When my attention returned to the stage, I saw Pearl was wearing a tall colorful hat decorated with little plastic bananas. It was made from things she had collected on Trash Truck Tuesdays, and she called it her Let's Go Bananas Hat.

"Hey, everybody! It's time to go bananas!"

She started hopping up and down with her hat flopping wildly from side to side.

"What did the farmer get when he crossed a refrigerator with a robot?"

"We don't know!" we replied.

"I don't know either, but it keeps the lettuce nice and crisp while it goes outside to…"

Then we all called out as loudly as we could, "Feed the chickens!"

Pearl ended her show with a high-kicking, foot-waggling dance she called The Dipsy Doodle.

"There's more than one kind of dancing in Paris," she said. "So maybe there's more than one way to be a chicken!"

The Mysterious Bottle Cap Lady

The next morning after the big show, Amelia let Pearl go down the chicken ladder first. It was the only kindness she received the whole day. The show had gone better than she had planned, but nothing had changed for her. She was still just not-so-good, not-so-normal Pearl. At breakfast, she grabbed a perfect piece of lettuce Blanche had been eyeing and chittered happily. Yes, there would always be Blanche, she told herself.

One evening when everyone else had gone up to roost for the night, Blanche and Pearl stayed behind. Blanche did not want anyone to see she was not feeling well and might struggle going up the ladder. Everyone needs to be strong and able to defend the flock against predators.

The two of them heard a soft scraping and dragging sound on the metal wire of the door to their run. When they turned around, they saw an opossum showing its teeth and hissing.

Blanche spread out her wings and ruffled her feathers to look her biggest and bravest, but the opossum did not back down. Blanche lunged forward to attack, but just as she did, her left leg buckled. Her body hit the ground with a loud, painful thud, and her wings sprawled out helplessly.

Then without thinking, Pearl jumped between the opossum and Blanche, but she did not attack. The opossum had not backed down for Blanche, and Pearl was much smaller.

She only knew one thing to do. She began hopping around on one foot while shaking the other foot right in the opossum's face.

"Trick or treat! Smell my feet! Do-Dah! Do-Dah! Do the Dipsy Doodle with me!"

The opossum took a step backwards.

Pearl did not know what would happen next, but at least she had bought them a few more minutes of life. She just kept singing and dancing until the confused opossum finally gave up.

Blanche recovered, and then the two of them took turns pecking the opossum's naked rear end as it climbed back up the wire fencing and out through a gap in the loose tarp roof.

"I wish the others had seen what you did. You saved us all," said Blanche. "They probably heard but thought you were just being silly. None of them believe silliness can ever save a chicken's life."

"I know," said Pearl. "But if they had seen me, they would have also seen you stumble and found out you are sick. That would not be good at all. They only put up with me because sometimes I make them laugh. I'm not big and strong like you. As long as you know, that's what matters to me."

When they headed up the ladder, it was almost completely dark. Gracie adjusted her feathers and nudged the others to make room for Blanche and Pearl. "Rest well," she told them.

This was different. No one ever had good wishes for them at bedtime except me. Pearl wondered if maybe Gracie had seen what had happened. She would ask her in private the next day when she had a chance, but that chance never came.

The next morning, Blanche was not herself. She was having a hard time walking and had no appetite. It was almost what you might expect from an old chicken, but she had not yet reached her second hatchday.

I carefully moved Blanche to the smaller coop and run, and brought Pearl over to join her. Blanche was fine with being in their old home because it was a more restful place to get well, but Pearl did not like it. She called it Chicken Jail. She didn't know when she would ever be able to put on another real comedy show. She seemed to be all out of plans for a wonderful new life.

Being back in their old home also bothered Pearl because The Bottle Cap Lady would often stand at the edge of our driveway and watch them. Pearl wasn't sure why this bothered her, but it did. The Bottle Cap Lady probably meant no harm, but she was definitely mysterious.

No one remembered her real name any more. Everyone called her The Bottle Cap Lady because she collected bottle caps from trash cans. Sometimes they had prizes printed on them, and the prizes gave her hope for a wonderful new life. At least, that is what she had told me once a long time ago.

Almost every day she would roam around the neighborhood and act as if she was playing Hide And Seek and looking for someone who wasn't there anymore. Pearl was glad she had Blanche for playing games. It seemed like The Bottle Cap Lady had no one.

She had been a waitress at The Chicken Place Restaurant which has been a landmark in our neighborhood for many years. It still has a huge statue of a white chicken perched on its roof which has withstood many hurricanes and nor'easters. Except for its red tail feathers, the statue looked like Blanche and Pearl, and maybe that is why she was so fascinated with the two of them.

Sometimes when The Bottle Cap Lady roamed around the neighborhood, she would wear her old waitress uniform with its matching lace-trimmed apron and fancy frilly hat. Pearl liked The Bottle Cap Lady's waitress hat.

When The Bottle Cap Lady dressed up as if she was still a waitress, she would often pretend to carry a big tray of food. It seemed to wobble from side to side, and then she would drop it and make a huge mess everywhere. She would make silly faces while trying to clean it all up. Afterwards she would sing a song and dance around in a circle while flapping her arms like she was a chicken. Neither Blanche nor Pearl understood imaginary food, but they did enjoy it when she would sing and dance.

Pearl began to wonder if what really bothered her most about The Bottle Cap Lady was how much the two of them were alike and how they both seemed to need just a simple everyday miracle.

Under The Camellias

As the weather turned colder, it became clear Blanche was truly sick. She ate less and spent more time to herself. Sitting in the warm winter sun seemed to help her the most. Cloudy days were tough for her, and Pearl watched over her more carefully.

Together the three of us learned the importance of being grateful for lovingkindness, for friendship, and for whatever small joys came our way. Each day was a gift to be treasured.

Pearl took care of Blanche better than anyone ever could. She would only eat after Blanche had eaten. She tried to not have any calamities or mishaps. Only occasionally would Pearl think about being a comedian or telling jokes or painting her toenails or wearing silly hats.

Sometimes they would play Who Can Stay Still The Longest? even though Pearl never won because she would see something to go off and explore. It had always been difficult for her to sit still anyway, and Pearl knew Blanche needed time alone to rest.

The pictures she collected on Trash Truck Tuesdays showed things that made people smile. Nothing made her smile more than Blanche, and so while Blanche rested, Pearl learned to draw pictures of the two of them together.

She studied the lines and dots that made up her favorite pictures. She could not figure out how people had made them, but she was sure she could make lines and dots almost just like people did.

Each of her drawings was created with the simplest materials she could find including some brought to her by the songbirds. Her pens and brushes were feathers and frayed twigs. Her inks were charred wood, mud, berry juice, or whatever else she could find to mix with sticky sap.

With practice, her lines grew more steady and sure. Those always came first. Then she filled in her favorite shapes with color. Finally she made dot patterns. She liked that part best. Making dots was like pecking for food, up and down, up and down.

Every now and then while Blanche slept, Pearl would spread out all her drawings and tell herself, "This is my life. This is my heart."

Because of Pearl's tender nursing, Blanche was able to make it through winter to enjoy the spring crocuses and daffodils in our garden.

One day, Blanche unexpectedly asked Pearl to put on a silly hat and tell some jokes. "Do a show just for me, will you?" she said. "It may make me feel better. Please."

Pearl was delighted. "I will, Blanche! I will! It will be like the old days. Then you will feel so much better. You'll see!"

Pearl rummaged through the treasures she had collected on Trash Truck Tuesdays. She made a new hat like those she had seen in pictures of nurses. She added a toy thermometer and two tongue depressors and called it her Get Well Soon Hat. Her favorite part was a plastic stethoscope wrapped in long flowing gold fringe and fancy metallic ribbon. She planned to wrap it around Blanche and maybe even tickle her with it.

As Blanche and I sat together and watched the show, she scooted closer to me, and I scooted closer to her. That was when I understood why Pearl enjoyed leaning against Blanche so much. Even though she was not at her best, she still felt solid and dependable.

Pearl added some new comedy material to her old jokes. Even though she had been holding back her silliness for so long, she had not lost her talent for delighting an audience.

Blanche laughed like she had when they were both baby chicks even though it seemed to hurt her sides. She knew how much Pearl missed having an audience and performing. Perhaps allowing others to give to us is a gift we give to them.

One day soon afterwards, Pearl said, "The songbirds told me everyone has flags with baby chicks, eggs, and white flowers in their front yards. Why is that? And why don't we have any? Is it because you have us here already in the backyard?"

"Those are called Easter eggs," I said.

"What kind of bird is this Easter Bird? I don't think I've ever seen one. Is it a kind of chicken?"

"There is no Easter Bird, but there is an Easter Bunny. And before you ask, bunnies do not lay eggs."

Pearl laughed because that is exactly what she was going to ask next.

"To tell you the truth, it's not easy to explain, but I think the flag pictures mean Love makes all things new because a baby chick is just about the newest thing there is. The white flowers are lilies, and they are clean and pure and new."

"Blanche's feathers are the biggest and whitest. Do you think Love will make Blanche new?" she asked hopefully.

"Love makes all things new, Pearl. But sometimes death has to happen first."

Blanche left us that Easter Sunday when it was just the two of them alone together. Out of the kindness in her heart, she had struggled to stay with us for as long as she could. She knew how lost Pearl would be without her.

When I got home from church and realized what had happened, I wrapped Blanche in soft cotton and found a nice place for her in our garden under the camellias.

And so together we hold in our hearts The Promise Of Easter, the promise that Love makes all things new.

No More Jokes To Tell

After Blanche left us, it seemed like a good time for Pearl to rejoin the others, but she was not ready. Even when I told her, "At a time like this, you all need each other," she just shook her head and looked over at Blanche's favorite spot.

Pearl hoped Gracie had seen what had happened with the opossum and had told the others, but she did not want to be away from where she had spent time together with Blanche. She wanted to stay close to her hidden treasures, especially her Get Well Soon Hat with Blanche's sweet smell still on it.

In the mornings, Pearl would stand at the top of their chicken ladder and cry out for Blanche, calling her home for breakfast. Then in the evenings, she would stand on their roost, and cry out again for Blanche, calling her home for bedtime. Filling the time in between was her most difficult challenge each day. Pearl wanted to believe Blanche would come back.

"If only I was a good normal chicken like the others, none of this would have happened," she told me one evening.

"Pearl, that's not true. Sometimes things happen that we can't explain. We can only hope maybe one day we might be able to understand. Until then we still have each other, even if it is just you and me. Do you think that will be enough?"

She sadly nodded her head, and we said our goodnights. She was glad she had taken time to draw pictures of Blanche in her heart. The ones she had made on scraps of paper were nice, but she could only see them in daylight. Eventually they would become old and faded. She could see the pictures in her heart anytime, and they would always be safe there.

The next evening, Pearl asked me, "Why do you love Gracie so much? Your voice is different with her. So is the way you move."

These are things I had not noticed about myself. Pearl could be a silly little hen, but she is also a serious observer, just as all comedians are.

"What is her trick? What did she do to make you love her so much? I never heard her tell any jokes, not a single one ever. She doesn't even wear silly hats."

"Maybe it's not more. Maybe it's just different. But I am beginning to love you in the same different way. The two of you are very similar."

Pearl tilted her head questioningly. This was hard for her to believe.

"I love Gracie the way I do because she has always had that lump on her side. She was always very timid and shy because of it as a baby chick. It has kept her from doing many of the things she wants to do. But she keeps dancing ballet even if it hurts sometimes. She still does all she can to enjoy her life.

"Do you remember the day when Bessie defended all of you against the stray cat? The top of her head was clawed, and I still remember how upset she was when she told me about what had happened. Her comb grew crooked and floppy afterwards. Some people would say it makes her look ugly. But when I look at her, I only see how brave she is and how much she loves all of you."

Pearl grew restless.

"I don't understand how any of that makes me like them," she protested. "I don't have a lump on my side. My comb is as straight as my feathers are white. I am a practically perfect little hen. You have just as much said so yourself before."

"Yes, I know. But when Blanche died, it was like a wound to your heart. No one can see your wound, but it is there. And it still hurts. But you are learning to keep going even though the scar on your heart reminds you of unpleasant things."

She looked down at her breast. She saw the pure white feathers on the outside. She felt her broken heart on the inside, but it did not scare her any longer.

"I am out of jokes and silly hats and silly anything. How can you still love me?"

"I love you all the more, Pearl, when you have nothing to give except your heart. Love covers imperfections. Love fills emptiness."

She looked into my eyes, hoping what I had told her was the truth.

"Do you think those little fireflies are like that too? When I tell them my very-best-ever-never-fail jokes, they don't laugh. Even when I dress up funny for them, they don't laugh.

"But when I cluck 'Bawk. Bawk. Bwawk-a-Bock,' they make a 'Blink. Blink. Blink-a-Blonk' with their lights."

"What do you think that means, Pearl?"

"I think it means and I hope it means they love me even if they don't understand my jokes."

"Do you feel the emptiness in your heart being filled?"

"Yes, I think so."

"Then that is certainly love. And the best kind of love, the same kind of love Blanche had for you. The fireflies love you even though you have nothing to give them in return."

We said our goodnights, and Pearl stood by herself and waited for her new friends, the fireflies, to come out.

A Wondrous Place

When the season of fireflies ended, Pearl felt her world getting smaller. She had been by herself for so long.
    One late autumn day, while I was raking leaves, Pearl watched intently, pacing back and forth to see if I raked up anything she

might want. While doing all of that pacing, she discovered a little gap in the fencing of her run area. She looked at it. She saw me looking at her looking at it. She did not say anything. She knew I would fix it if she did. I went back to my raking.

Pearl decided she had to remember the little gap. Maybe Blanche had only been playing Who Can Stay Still The Longest? with her. Maybe she had already found the little gap and was out exploring the world and playing Hide And Seek.

"When are we going to put out The Big Blue Hippopotamus?" she asked. "And the other decorations? I will be glad to help you. The songbirds told me about them. They said we must have some like the other people are putting out because we don't have a hippopotamus in our backyard like we had chickens in the backyard at Easter. Once we have them all put out, then maybe you can explain Christmas to me. The songbirds couldn't."

"Pearl, we don't need to have decorations to celebrate Christmas either," I said because I wasn't sure what else to say. How do you explain Christmas to a chicken?

"I will need to find out more about The Big Blue Hippopotamus and this thing called Christmas."

"Yes, of course," I said and went back to raking leaves. Along with forgetting about the gap in Pearl's fencing, I had also forgotten how unstoppably curious she could be.

Pearl began slipping through the little gap in her fencing to explore. She would hide under the bushes in front of the house and study what she could see of the decorations and colorful lights in the front yards along our street. Sometimes she stayed out all night long without me ever knowing it. The days were shorter. It was still dark when I left for work and dark when I got home. In the mornings, I thought she was laying an egg in her nesting box. In the evenings, I thought she had gone up to roost.

Then one night she noticed tiny golden-white lights flashing on and off in a pattern a few houses away from ours. She was almost sure they were her firefly friends from the summer, but she would have to leave our yard to get a better look.

The next day, Pearl made a Reindeer Antlers Hat to wear so she could disguise herself as a Christmas decoration. If anyone came along, she would play Who Can Stay Still The Longest? until they passed by. As soon as it became dark enough, she quickly headed for the yard with the most lights. Surely whoever lived there had to know the most about Christmas.

When Pearl reached the flashing lights, she was amazed. They were not fireflies at all. They were strings of lights just like the ones for her comedy show, but there were dozens of them with many more sizes and colors than she could have ever imagined.

And there were decorations everywhere! They were all arranged as if they were telling stories. Most were old like the things she collected on Trash Truck Tuesdays, but under the lights, they looked amazing. Surely someone as special as Blanche had to be in such a wondrous place.

Pearl wandered slowly through the decorations, trying to figure out what stories they were telling. She found a plywood cutout of The Big Blue Hippopotamus. It wasn't new or made of plastic like the one next door to our house, but this one had pink toenails just like Pearl had when she performed in her own real comedy show so long ago. This was a very good sign. Blanche had to be somewhere close by.

Just as Pearl was ready to call out for Blanche, the front door opened. Someone stepped out onto the porch and sat in a rocking chair. It was The Bottle Cap Lady! She smelled like cookies.

Pearl knew what she had to do. Surely The Bottle Cap Lady could tell her about Christmas. She might even tell her where Blanche was or at least help find her.

Pearl adjusted her Reindeer Antlers Hat. Then she hurried up the front sidewalk, stood politely at the bottom of the porch steps, and waited.

When The Bottle Cap Lady noticed her, Pearl clucked and bwawked cheerfully and then motioned with her wing toward the most colorful group of decorations.

The Bottle Cap Lady did not understand, but Pearl would not give up. She started pecking around the decorations one at a time. She was careful not to damage or knock over anything.

Finally Pearl pecked around the plastic nativity scene. It was the only one on the whole block, and so it didn't seem to be particularly important. Pearl liked it though. The stable was shaped a little like her own coop, and there was a kind of nesting box with straw. There was no chicken or egg in it, just a little baby. He had outstretched hands which always means food to any chicken, especially to Blanche who liked to eat.

Maybe Christmas was about The Little Baby With Outstretched Hands feeding everybody in the whole world. That would certainly be something worth celebrating.

Pearl must have finally stumbled onto a real clue because at last The Bottle Cap Lady said, "You want to know about Christmas, don't you, Little Sweetie?"

Pearl stopped pecking, gave her best smile, and went back to the front porch steps. So The Bottle Cap Lady moved her rocking chair closer and began to tell Pearl about Christmas.

"I ain't nothing," she said. "I'm just an old nobody going nowhere with nothing." She thought this was as good a place as any to start, and what would a chicken be able to understand anyway?

"Lots of people might wonder why I drag out all this junk every year. They see the ragged decorations with burned out bulbs and old faded plastic stuff nobody else would ever want. They see the homemade plywood decorations and the different strings of lights that don't match. But this, this is like my church out here on my front porch. My church.

"You probably don't know anything about church now, do you? Well, there's something you and I have in common! They wouldn't want either one of us in there. Me, I smell like old soda pop bottles. You, Little Sweetie, well, you smell like a chicken!"

The Bottle Cap Lady and Pearl laughed together. For a moment, The Bottle Cap Lady thought maybe this little white hen with the silly hat might really know exactly what she was saying. But that would take a miracle, and The Bottle Cap Lady was sure there were no more miracles left in her life.

"I don't know what it is, but when all of these lights are glowing, it just makes me feel good. Sometimes I will stay out here the whole night just looking at everything. People don't bother you at night. They don't stare at you or talk about you when they think you can't hear them at night. They don't tell you what you ought to do. Or ought not to do. These Christmas lights are just about my only friends."

She pointed to the empty roof of the nativity scene stable. "It used to have an angel up on the top there, but when it lost its halo, I took it down and put it with the others. It's not The Christmas Angel if it don't have a halo. You know, with them white feathers, you're a little like an angel yourself."

There was a long silence. Pearl tilted her head to listen for what was next.

"My baby, my Judy Lynne, she was The Christmas Angel in the Christmas pageant a long time ago, the last one I ever went to. The Christmas Angel is the only angel of all the angels up there with words to recite. Everyone said she was the prettiest angel they ever had.

"How I wish I could see her in that pageant just one more time."

Pearl had seen the group of plastic angels in the yard. An angel must have a body like a little girl and wings like a chicken.

"You know what? Sometimes the ugliest people have the prettiest little babies. At least that's how it worked out with my baby, my Judy Lynne.

"You're so pretty, and you don't got no babies, do you? You'd be a good little Chicken Momma. I just know you would. Some of us girls just ain't meant to be mommas, and some of us is meant to be mommas for only a little while. Bless them that's meant to be mommas until the day they die."

She looked back up at the empty roof of the nativity scene stable and then down at Pearl.

"You'd better get home now. He's going to wonder where you are if you're not home."

Pearl flapped her wings and did a few dance steps to show her gratitude. Then she hurried away with a new unexplainable joy in her heart.

Secrets And Presents

Early one morning, Pearl listened as The Big Boy from the end of the street explained Christmas to The Little Boy from the end of the street. The Big Boy had a Big Blue Hippopotamus in his yard, so he must know a lot about Christmas too.

"Don't be stupid. It's almost Christmas Eve night. Then Santa Claus will bring my new go-cart and fill my stocking with candy. If you haven't made your list, you'd better do it now, right now. If you don't, you get leftovers nobody else wants. If you're not in bed and asleep, you get nothing."

"So what do I put on my list?"

"How should I know, you little goof!"

"I'd like a puppy. That's what I'd really like."

"You don't want a puppy on your list. Put a new bicycle. You can always get a puppy. People are giving them away all the time. You don't see anybody giving away free bicycles, do you?"

"No, I guess you're right."

"I know I'm right."

They went off to throw rocks in the little creek across from our house. Pearl felt lucky to have learned so much so quickly about Christmas.

You make a list of what you want most. But it has to have only special things, not everyday free things. You must be home on Christmas Eve, and you must be asleep when Santa Claus comes. When you wake up on Christmas morning, you have everything on your list. This was the best plan ever!

Pearl took out her favorite drawing. It showed Blanche and herself smiling happily together. This was what Pearl wanted more than anything. Having Blanche back home was much more special than a go-cart or a bicycle. And what would a chicken do with either one of those anyway? Pearl tried to imagine herself riding a bicycle and laughed.

She decided to send her treasured drawing to Santa so he would know exactly what she wanted for Christmas. She just needed to add some words.

She made some red ink from her breakfast pomegranate pips and used one of her old feathers as a pen. Then she made marks on her paper like when she was drawing pictures. She loved making marks. These marks would give her a wonderful new life when Santa brought Blanche back home.

She decided it would be best to use as few words as possible. Word marks were not as easy to make as picture marks.

Dear Santa

Please

Blanche

Pumpkin Seeds

Love

Pearl

She rolled up the paper so it would fit through the fencing and called the songbirds to come and get it for delivery. They would take it as far north as they could and then the snowy owls would take it the rest of the way to Santa Claus.

She looked especially content when I sat down with her to read the newspaper.

"What are you so happy about today, Pearl?" I asked.

"Secrets and presents."

"I see. So you finally figured out what The Big Blue Hippopotamus and the other decorations are all about?"

Pearl nodded happily.

"Well, listen. You don't really need to give me a gift. I will be plenty happy watching you enjoy a special Christmas gift I've made for you."

Pearl looked at me questioningly. I thought it was because she was trying to figure out what my present for her would be, but she was actually wondering about giving gifts.

The Big Boy had not said anything about giving gifts, only getting them. Maybe every time somebody gets a gift there has to be a different somebody who gives a gift.

Pearl decided she would give The Bottle Cap Lady a gift. She could not imagine anyone else giving her a gift. Her only friends were Christmas lights.

Maybe people had always picked on her and told her, "Why can't you just be a good normal Bottle Cap Lady?" Pearl knew what that was like.

And even if The Bottle Cap Lady didn't have a gift for Pearl, it would be fine. Pearl's best gift was coming from Santa Claus. He would be bringing Blanche back home along with piles of roasted pumpkin seeds.

Pearl would make a new angel halo for The Bottle Cap Lady so she could put her big plastic angel back up on the stable roof. That's exactly what she would do.

The Most Silent Pearl Ever

Early that Christmas Eve morning, Pearl began making her gift for The Bottle Cap Lady. She pulled out some thin wire, flexible enough for her to bend and shape and braid and wrap with her beak. She had learned how to do a great many clever things with her beak, and even though the wire did not taste good, she did not let it bother her.

She looked through her stash of treasures and pulled out all the sparkling glittery metallic things she had collected to turn into hats and costumes just in case she was ever able to have another comedy show. But there were not enough of them.

It was Tuesday, Trash Truck Day. Pearl waited all morning, but the trash truck never came. She counted and counted again on her toes. Six toes. Six days. Then it was always Trash Truck Day. She did not know about holiday schedules. There would be no new sparkling or shiny things to collect that Christmas Eve.

Pearl poked and probed into the deepest and most protected part of her special corner. She pulled out her Get Well Soon Hat with its long golden fringe and ribbons. It reminded her of how Blanche had smiled that day, one of the last smiles Blanche had ever given her.

She knew she would have to take it apart if she was ever going to make her gift for The Bottle Cap Lady. She smelled the last of Blanche's sweet feathery fragrance, gave up her one last greatest treasure, and quickly finished her work.

There was no time to wonder if it was the right thing to do or to have any regrets. Sometimes you have to be a foolishly extravagant and generous giver, she told herself. Sometimes you have to sacrifice an irreplaceable good thing for an even better good thing.

As the sun began to set, Pearl hurried to The Bottle Cap Lady's house. She would give her the angel halo and then quickly get back home before I returned from work. Then she would be on her roost in her coop and asleep before Santa Claus arrived with Blanche and roasted pumpkin seeds.

"If you're not at home in your own bed and asleep, you get nothing." That was what The Big Boy from the end of the street had said. Pearl did not want to forget. On Christmas morning, she would wake up beside Blanche. Then they would feast on roasted pumpkin seeds, and she would not need anything else.

But when Pearl got to The Bottle Cap Lady's house, she was already sitting in her rocking chair. She was looking up at the empty stable roof and crying. Pearl put the angel halo at the bottom of the steps. Everything in the yard seemed so bright and happy, but The Bottle Cap Lady's heart did not.

Pearl flapped her wings and bwawked cheerfully like before, but The Bottle Cap Lady would not look at her. She just kept looking up at the empty top of the stable and crying. Maybe she has a wound on her heart too, thought Pearl.

Then Pearl had her most brilliant idea ever. She would be The Bottle Cap Lady's Christmas Angel.

She adjusted the halo she had made to fit her own head. It had to be a lot smaller, and she had to take off several large pieces of her precious golden fringe that reminded her of Blanche. Then with her new Angel Halo Hat sparkling in the

Christmas lights, she flew to the top of the nativity stable and spread out her wings exactly as the plastic angels did.

The more Pearl's white feathers reflected the light, the more The Little Baby With The Outstretched Hands seemed to glow.

"Is that you, Judy Lynne?" asked The Bottle Cap Lady as she wiped away her tears. "Oh, my goodness, aren't you just the prettiest Christmas Angel ever? Yes, you are, my sweet little Judy Lynne.

"You know you ought to not be playing Hide And Seek like that right before the Christmas pageant. I've been looking absolutely everywhere for you, for days and days, so many I can't count, I've been looking everywhere for you."

She wiped away the last of her tears.

"Now listen, Momma's going to take a little nap before it's time to leave for the pageant. Don't you go off playing no more Hide And Seek. I love you so much, my sweet little Judy Lynne."

She closed her eyes.

This was not what Pearl had expected. She was not Judy Lynne. She was not a little girl. She was a chicken, a not-so-good, not-so-normal chicken named Pearl. But then she remembered how The Bottle Cap Lady had said she wanted to see her little girl as The Christmas Angel just one more time. Pearl also remembered the game called Who Can Stay Still The Longest? from when Blanche had been sick. It was the hardest game Blanche ever tried to teach her. Pearl never won, but she had to win this time. Somehow she was giving The Bottle Cap Lady something no one else could give her. Suddenly Pearl was glad to be exactly who she was.

Pearl heard more sobs. She wanted to cry too, but she knew she shouldn't. It was not her time to cry. She was doing this for The Bottle Cap Lady, not for herself.

"Judy Lynne, Sweetie Girl," The Bottle Cap Lady called out. "You are so precious to me. Just look at my pretty girl."

Then she seemed to wake up, and she started speaking to Pearl.

"You know, the last Christmas pageant I ever went to was the one my Judy Lynne was in as The Christmas Angel. She was the prettiest angel they ever had.

"Some people say when a child dies, it's because God needs another little angel. But that's not in the Bible book they gave my baby. Did you know that? I looked. I looked real hard. It's not in there."

Then after a long pause, The Bottle Cap Lady began talking to her little girl again.

"Judy Lynne, Sweetie, after the program is over, we'll go home, and Momma will make you some hot chocolate milk just the way you like it with those soft little marshmallows and maybe one really big one right in the middle. Because you are so special to me. Oh, Honey Girl, you are so special and so pretty and so beautiful to your Momma."

Her voice softened more and more and then she was talking to Pearl again. "At Christmas, I can forget my troubles. Mostly. At least they don't seem so bad. When I'm out here with all the lights on, I don't feel so alone anymore. You see, I'm not the only one who lost their pretty little baby. God lost his pretty little baby too."

Pearl was as still as Pearl had ever been.

"Thinking about that little baby born all those years ago in a stable makes me believe one day it's all going to be made right somehow. It's way beyond me to make it turn out that way on my own. But I have to believe that little baby can do it. If I don't believe that, what do I have?" she asked. "What do I have?" Her voice trailed off as if not expecting an answer. Maybe she was just asking herself.

"The rest of Christmas, like the Santa Claus and the reindeer and the lights, those are all just fillers until everything is made right one day by that little baby."

Pearl wanted to say something, but she didn't know what. She felt as if a door had been opened and somehow she understood Christmas in a way words could never express.

She did not know how long she had been standing there. It had to be way past bedtime, but she did not mind. She felt a new kind of love flowing into her heart and then flowing out again to The Bottle Cap Lady's heart.

Surely this was what Blanche had tried to tell her about Light and Life and Love being all about giving. And surely this was how the fireflies had loved her when she had nothing to give them but her heart.

From time to time, The Bottle Cap Lady would wake up. Sometimes she would be more awake than other times and would say something about Christmas, but mostly she would just say, "Judy Lynne. I love you, Sweetie Girl."

Sometimes her breathing would become heavy and labored. Sometimes it was as soft and easy as if she was a little baby herself.

A Happy Merry Christmas

Finally as the first rays of the morning sunlight were showing over the treetops, The Bottle Cap Lady stirred awake.

"What's the matter, Sweetie Girl? Did you forget your lines? I will say them for you. 'Glory to God in the highest, and on earth, peace and goodwill.' All because that little baby was born to make everything right."

By then, Pearl understood Christmas as well as any chicken could.

She was able to see the ground and flew down. She stretched out her legs and her wings. It felt good, very good. At last, she must have won the game called Who Can Stay Still The Longest? when it mattered most.

She hurried past the decorations and up the walkway and hopped into The Bottle Cap Lady's lap. It was all she knew to do so The Bottle Cap Lady would understand she had a best friend, even if her best friend was only a chicken.

"Well, Happy Merry Christmas to you, Little Lady!" she said. "Your name is Pearl, isn't it, Sweetie? I think that's what I've heard him call you."

Pearl nodded.

"That's a good name for you, Sweetie. A real good name. You are so precious, a precious little treasure is what you are. And if that's not your name, it should be because you are just as white and beautiful and pure and good as any pearl I've ever seen, real or dime-store-make-believe."

They smiled at each other. Pearl settled into the nest of The Bottle Cap Lady's lap. It was soft and warm.

"I know you've been looking for your friend, that other white one like you. I think I just may help you look for her, maybe one day real soon. I don't know what her name is, but I will know her when I see her.

"I have a feeling I already know where she is. She is probably in the same place where my Judy Lynne is. They might be playing together right now. Don't you worry though. My Judy Lynne is real gentle with everybody and everything.

"So don't you worry. I'll find her. I'll find them both. And then we will all wait for you to come and join us. I promise. It won't be long. The waiting goes a lot faster than you might think."

She looked far away off beyond the decorations and the houses and the trees to the morning sunrise colors. They reminded her of beautiful glass Christmas ornaments as they spread their newness across everything, even herself.

"Maybe life isn't so much about getting yourself loved. Maybe life is about being with Love. That's what I'm going to go find out for us, Sweetie."

She laid her hand on Pearl's back and stroked her feathers. Then The Bottle Cap Lady carefully lifted Pearl up to her cheek.

"I'll bet you don't know my name. I know everybody calls me The Bottle Cap Lady, but I have a real name, just like you." Then she whispered her name into Pearl's ear.

It was a secret. It was a secret just like the ones Pearl and Blanche had shared together. What a wonderful gift, she thought. Now she knew The Bottle Cap Lady was her friend for sure.

"It's a name that means what we are to each other, Sweetie. You'd better run along home now. He's going to be missing you, and I hope he's got some real nice Christmas presents for you to open up this morning. Thank you, Pearl."

Pearl knew she had already been given the best gift. She bwawked and clucked and did a joyfully silly dance down The Bottle Cap Lady's front sidewalk.

"Thank you for giving me my dream, Pearl," the Bottle Cap Lady called to her one last time. "And for helping me draw a picture in my heart to hold safe forever."

At the end of the street, Pearl could see The Big Boy putting gas into his new go-cart and the Little Boy trying to ride his new bicycle. Santa Claus had visited their houses. They had been at home and asleep. But Pearl had not.

There would be no roasted pumpkin seeds in her stocking. There would be no Blanche to lean against for comfort. But somehow it did not matter. She still felt the same Love she had felt the night before, the kind of Love that only comes from Forever, the kind of Love that lasts Forever.

And so Pearl took out the picture she had made in her own heart of The Promise Of Easter, the promise that Love makes all things new.

Then she made another picture in her heart of The Promise Of Christmas, the promise that Love gives its very best even to those who have nothing to give in return.

And just like that, without her even knowing it, while Pearl hopped, skipped, and stumbled into her own backyard, it happened.

It happened as quietly as a tiny white feather falling on fresh Christmas snow.

The wonderful new life Pearl had been wanting for so long began without her even being aware.

Perhaps that is just the way it is when you receive a simple everyday miracle.

How To Explain Christmas To Chickens

About The Author

John Spiers is a writer, artist, and guardian to a small flock of chickens who live in the center of his backyard garden.

While he often produced small writing and drawing projects over the years, he never found his creative purpose until he decided to raise some baby chicks. They became the characters in his stories and the subjects of his drawings.

His work seeks to share the same joy he feels when spending time with his chickens along with bits of "chicken wisdom" about life which he has learned from them.

About This Book

The author enjoys hiding things in his illustrations, and his chickens enjoy finding them. Perhaps you will as well.

If you are as curious and persistent as Pearl, you can find a pair of Gracie's ballet slippers that he promised to put in every book. You will also find three friendship hearts and The Bottle Cap Lady's real name.

It may help your search if you imagine sitting with the author and his chickens in their garden home where there is always room for one more friend.

MyLifeWithGracie.com

CPSIA information can be obtained
at www.ICGtesting.com
Printed in the USA
BVHW010934050123
655628BV00020B/463